Alien

Champion's

Bride

I0634876

Taylor Neptune

ISBN: 978-1-63481-055-5

Politics

Zhanshi

"How about that imperial candidate?"

"Do you really think that he can rule the Intergalactic Federation properly? We might be separate sovereign planets under one big aegis, but the imperial station still wields a lot of power. I think that he would focus on interplanetary commerce, to the benefit of every citizen of the Intergalactic Federation, but I have to admit that his stance towards accepting new planets into the Federation leaves a whole lot to be desired. His mother was Alban, so it's not as if he doesn't have a drop of new blood, but he seems very hostile to new people and expanding our reach."

"Well, who do you want to take the imperial station?"

"I'd really prefer that we see our first female emperor...empress, I suppose...or our first Yahadun emperor, whose father was Galixian. I really think that they have a shot."

"We'll see which way the wind blows. I can't imagine someone with such strong protectionist policies taking over the Federation. Inside of the Federation, we might prosper, but our relations with planets who haven't yet joined would become quite strained."

Zhanshi opened his mouth to speak about the political matters of the day, but his father immediately cut him off.

"I'll never vote for an empress. Women have no place running things. Too emotional. Can you imagine?"

Zhanshi watched as his father's friends all laughed and nodded. They didn't believe that a woman could hold a position of

huge responsibility and power.
Zhanshi knew that he needed to
keep his mouth shut, but anger
burned in his gut. Women were far
less common than men in the
universe, but he thought that a
woman, the right woman, could do
a good job. He didn't know if the
current would-be empress was the
right woman — she might not be —
but he'd like to see a female
empress in his lifetime. It wouldn't
happen as long as people like his

father and his cronies were part of the voting electorate.

Zhanshi found it ironic that during a lavish dinner which was supposed to be celebrating his own victory in the sparring ring, his father took over. Like always. Zhanshi had found attention and fame because of his fighting prowess, but outside of the ring, he was just a crown prince who didn't have much say in anything.

"The Yahadun doesn't have any

defense experience."

Zhanshi jumped in, "But there's a space militia that is supporting..."

He trailed off after his father glared at him fiercely. "Nobody wants to hear about his rag-tag space militia. The Yahadun cannot keep us safe."

Yet again, all of his father's friends nodded in unison. Zhanshi gave up. He didn't know why he even tried anymore. He waited a

—
8

few minutes, then he bowed to his dining companions before going up the stairs towards his quarters.

His feet took him past his quarters into the courtyard that his mother had cultivated. It was full of Oxitan flowers. There were cheap pink floating flowers, but his mother had somehow contrived to keep violettes double alive here. His father didn't know; if he had, he would've capitalized on it. But there were things that you did for money and other things that you did for love. His mother had never wanted to make a living off of her love for flowers. She hadn't kept much a secret from his dad, but the flowers were hers and hers alone. She loved beautiful things, even simple ones.

In contrast, his father had a calculator for a heart. Frowning, Zhanshi thought of the heart of the matter: his father would not permit him to do anything while there were more years for his father to continue building his power, wealth, and influence in the quadrant. Currently, Zhanshi was just an ornament, an afterthought. He knew that one day, he'd finally ascend to the throne. He'd be able to fix the kingdom and make it everything that it should be.

Until that day, he was just passing time.

Lounge

Zhanshi

"Oh!"

Zhanshi turned around to see a young woman enter the courtyard.

"I'm so sorry to disturb you, Prince Zhanshi." Her cheeks were flushed. "I just intended to collect some flowers to make my bedroom smell sweet. I had no idea that you'd be here, sir. I really enjoyed your victory tonight. The way that you laid him out cold was just inspiring."

Zhanshi noticed her beauty: the long, dark hair that flowed down to her waist, the close-cut silk dress cut to accentuate her curves, and the high slit of the dress up to her upper thigh, nearly getting to scandalous heights. She was probably a plant from his father, who was constantly pushing women on him, saying that he should get started on the future heirs. Zhanshi didn't want to fall into any traps, but he also wouldn't turn down time in the company of a pretty girl; his father didn't know him very well, but he knew enough.

"Would you like a drink? I just got a shipment of ruou from Dalat."

"I'd be honored, my prince."

"Come to my private lounge,"

he told her. It was an old routine, one that he'd pulled many times before. He was a champion and a prince — flashy on the outside no matter what the reality was — and he had no problems charming girls into his bedroom.

They walked out of the garden and headed towards his suite. He unlocked the door via a retina scan before holding the door open for his fan.

"After you," he said.

She walked past him and said, "Wow!" She stood and looked around his suite. "It's just so beautiful."

Zhanshi suppressed a sigh. He knew that he often got this reaction — and it probably helped him get lucky — but his bedroom was his bedroom. He'd never known any other life than the one that a prince of one of Zhongguo's kingdoms would know. He envied Xun, his distant cousin on his mother's side, who had left Zhongguo years ago and never looked back. Xun hadn't been in line for any thrones. He'd never sat through the stupid statecraft lessons that Zhanshi had been forced to memorize by heart. He wasn't forced to sit through state dinners like Zhanshi was.

"Let me pour you some ruou." He went to his small bar and opened the cold cabinet. He expertly poured the ruou.

"I've never had ruou before."

He brought two small shot glasses over to the girl and gave one to her.

"To new experiences." He lifted the glass.

"New experiences." She hit his glass with her own, making a soft clinking sound.

They both swallowed the alcohol. The girl coughed hard, turning red again.

What was he doing? He was

old enough to move on beyond the easy routine of taking women to bed just to pass time.

"How is the ruou?" he inquired.

"Really good. Very strong. The aftertaste..."

"Let me give you some xocolatl to wash it away."

He moved to the machine in the corner that dispensed his hot drinks. Xocolatl — the sweet drink that was spiced with peppermint and other things — was a great accompaniment to ruou.

He poured two mugs with xocolatl, which smelled absolutely great, the fresh scent filling his nose, before bringing them back to her.

"It's hot!"

He felt himself getting annoyed. Yes, she was a pretty girl, but she seemed quite simple-minded. He was also deeply suspicious that his father wanted him to mate with this particular girl, and in this case, he could defy his father's unusually subtle hint.

"It's best drunk very quickly," he said to nudge her to leave faster. He drained his mug in mere seconds.

She tried to imitate him only to spill xocolatl on herself, dark drops falling onto her silk dress. But then her mug was empty. She showed him the bottom of her cup. She was overly eager, which made alarm bells ring in his head.

Definitely a plant.

"Thank you for coming up to my suite. I'm quite tired after the fight, so I'm going to go to bed early."

She sat there, as if she hoped for an invitation into his bed. But he meant to actually go to sleep, so he got to his feet and opened the door that led to the outside hallway.

"Thank you for tonight."

He tried not to feel bad when

he watched her face fall. She'd obviously had higher hopes for tonight. In another time, another place, he'd have given her what she wanted. But she wanted the glamor, the flash, the handsome face and the athlete's body. She didn't want him, not really.

She scurried out of his suite, and he could see that she had begun to cry, making him feel like an utter heel. He should stop doing things like this; it would only upset girls and not really help him in any way. He closed the door after her and went into the sonic shower to clean up after his fight. He dried off and went into his bed, embraced by cold sheets. He needed to find something to do with his time that was actually worthwhile.

Sickness

Annaisha

Annaisha heard a slight thud at the door to her chamber.

"Come in," she called.

Her door opened, and her favorite AI bot came inside, wearing an expression of anguish on his silver nano-woven face, which was modeled off of a portrait of Annaisha's grandfather, who had died before she was born. He had the same wide cheekbones and tapering chin that Annaisha had and fierce eyebrows just like her grandfather had had. It was like having an echo of her grandfather taking care of her.

Her heart began to thump in her chest. Zip was always so composed, so something was seriously wrong.

Even though she could communicate telepathically with

her robots, the ones that she knew well, she normally resorted to vocalized speech. Her telepathy was patchy; some days, it worked just fine. Other days, it went on the fritz and none of the robots seemed to be able to hear her.

Out loud, she asked, "What's wrong, Zip?"

"Come with me."

Annaisha frowned. It wasn't like Zip to be cryptic. She followed him swiftly down the corridor to the party simulation room. When the door was opened, the AI miniatures in the party simulation began to dance.

But their movements were just a little bit too slow. She walked into the room and came close to the nearest miniature. It slowly turned its head to engage with her, but there was a small creak when its head turned. Zip was right; there definitely was something wrong.

If there was something making her AI slow down, it was not impacting Zip. She looked at him, her closest friend. Zip was okay, but the more Annaisha thought about it, it made sense. Zip was made from premium materials from the best engineers on Riben. His components were of much high quality than the silly little AI miniatures that she'd built and programmed herself. Her uncle had bought Zip with the greatest care, fully believing in her ability to run the family planetoid with a sufficient amount of help. He'd known that Annaisha would never be able to command a legion of Ribenren, so he'd helped her get on her feet with pricy AI.

Her eyebrows drew together. She fought off a little tendril of worry. Pushing past it, she asked Zip to inject the system with stabilizing code. It would take Annaisha a lot more time to program than it would take Zip. His processing capacity far exceeded her own, but he could only do what he was told and perform his pre-programmed tasks.

She watched as he moved to a terminal and code began to flash on the screen. She breathed a sigh of relief. This fast code injection should fix it. She wanted to believe it, anyway. The thought of her AI breaking down would ruin her mood.

Waiting was the hardest part. She didn't want to wait around for Zip to finish programming his smaller cousins. She left Zip to the repair job and went back to her own room and opened her cold cabinet; the stress made her reach for her sugary bubble tea.

She got one of her big straws out and added honey bubbles to the mix. The honey bubbles were kept in a small warming compartment; the mix between the cold tea and the warm bubbles made a delicious sensation.

She drank it down while she thought about what could possibly be going wrong with her bots. She took every precaution to keep her bots connected to a clean system. Any malfunction didn't make any sense. No virus of any kind should be able to enter, let alone infect her bots.

She heard another thump on

the door. Zip had come back.

"Is it done?"

Zip shook his head back and forth. "I couldn't fix it." She could see the clear disappointment on Zip's nano-woven face; who said that AI didn't have feelings? She knew that they did.

"It's okay," she told Zip, though she had to swallow down a big lump in her throat. "I'll just send them to the mechanic."

She went to her glow pad and

tapped the keys that would put her in contact with the mechanic that she used for big problems.

"Yes?" Her mechanic was very brusque, but he was one of the best people on Riben for what she needed.

"My small bots are sick, sir." He was the only person who could do a better job than she could with the bots that she'd built from scratch; it wouldn't do to offend him, and he was very crotchety.

"Bring 'em in. I've got some time this afternoon. I'll give you an estimate once I take a look."

"Thank you."

He clicked off the glow pad. Other people might consider him rude, but Annaisha was used to his personality. He just didn't have time for the small talk that other people did, because he considered it an absolute waste of time. Annaisha privately agreed, but she couldn't get away with the same degree of rudeness.

She went back to the party simulation room to collect her bots. Her heart squeezed painfully when she saw them turn to her. They were even slower than before, and Zip's fix obviously hadn't helped at all.

She collected all of them and put them in a large package to send to the mechanic, putting them on top of one of her largest hover carts. She could get a drone to take them down, but she didn't want to. She'd hire a levi-car and take the bots there herself. It wouldn't help her to sit in her chambers and brood over what could possibly be happening.

She was in luck when she went back to her room to use the glow pad to order a levi-car. There was one near her home, and it'd be there faster than she could even walk down the stairs with the bots on their big hover cart.

When she got to vehicle, she stuffed the bots through the door of the levi-car. She folded the hover cart down into a small size, and then she got in herself, desperately hoping that the mechanic would be able to fix her bots.

Research

Annaisha

By the time that the levi-car arrived at the mechanic's workshop, Annaisha's worry had grown like a supernova. She looked at her bots again. They were brilliantly engineered, if she did say so herself. The AI in their minds should be as sharp as when they were first put together. She might lose a little money from having to shut down her party simulation room, but the profit loss wasn't what she was worried about. She was more worried about what the mechanic might charge to get them back into working shape, because she'd pay any price to fix them.

The door of the levi-car opened. Annaisha got out and unfolded her hover cart before taking her bots back out of the levi-car.

When she got into the workshop, she saw that the mechanic was under a huge, hulking piece of machinery.

"Do the intake," he told her, still on the ground. "I'll get to it later."

Annaisha knew where his intake forms were. She'd done her own checks — and Zip had, too, of course — but she didn't have the same kind of equipment that the mechanic did.

She plugged the bots one by one into his diagnostic equipment. A confusing number of lines appeared on the terminal's screen; Annaisha couldn't read anything that it was spitting out. Whatever the mechanic had coded into this particular machine, it wasn't Standard.

When she was done with all of the bots, she stood up. She didn't say goodbye to the mechanic; he was still under the big machine, and she wouldn't disturb him. He wouldn't appreciate it. She knew where everything was, so she took her credit pass and put down a deposit of a thousand credits to handle her bots. He charged the highest prices on Riben. The cost of the repair would be very high. She'd just hope that when she re-opened the party simulation room, she'd be able to make it up.

She walked back to the levi-car waiting for her outside. Fighting back tears now that she was alone, she told it to take her home. She'd been taking care of her bots since she built them, and needing to take all of them to the mechanic was humiliating. She thought that she was pretty good at what she did, but she obviously didn't know everything that she needed to know.

Her feet felt as if she had lead weights attached to them as she got out of the levi-car and walked back into her home. Zip met her at the door.

She just shook her head at him and walked back up the stairs.

In her room, she saw her neglected bubble tea, the honey bubbles cold now. She wasn't in the mood for it anymore, so she threw it in the waste disposal bin.

She went to her terminal and began to research all the viruses that could possibly impact bots.

More Malfunctions

Annaisha

Six hours later, she was snapped out of her research by Zip's hand on her shoulder.

"Time to go to bed, Annaisha." Zip was her best friend but also her caretaker. He'd been programmed to take care of her when she wouldn't take care of herself.

She shook his hand off.

"I'm not done yet."

The amount of research that she'd done had been immense. She'd researched all of the possible AI illnesses with a particular focus on the newest ones to enter the quadrant. The number was shockingly large.

"It's late."

Annaisha looked at the clock.

"Stars above!"

It was nearly dawn.

Annaisha rubbed her eyes and yawned. Normally, her bullheadedness was an asset. Whatever the virus was, it was going to shut down part of her recreational park. She didn't believe that any of the owners of the nearest four recreational parks would stoop so low. Planeteers, all of her peers, tended to be classy folks, eager to help one another. She could probably ask for some of the party bots to be sent, if she really needed to. She'd do the same for any of them.

Her eyes felt like there were heavy weights attached to them. When she realized that her eyes had been closed for several minutes, she opened them and struggled to her feet. She put her terminal to sleep and went to her bed.

* * *

The next morning, she woke up to see Zip standing next to her.

"What is it, Zip?" Her voice was very low. She yawned and covered her mouth with her hand.

"It happened again."

She was instantly alert, the hairs on the back of her neck standing up. Her eyes flew wide open. She was definitely awake now.

"What do you mean?"

Instead of answering her, Zip took her in the opposite direction in the corridor to her dining hall.

Her dining bots were more expensive than her party bots, and she hadn't built them herself, not having specialized in any culinary areas.

She covered her mouth as she saw how sluggishly all of them were moving. She could see sparks coming from the neck of one.

Zip was right next to her with anti-static gloves, which would keep her protected from the worst of it. She went to the bot and rotated its head until she could see its insides. She frowned. Nothing technically seemed to be wrong, but she could very clearly see that something was.

"Let me take off your head, Zip," she commanded. She turned to him and performed the same procedure. There wasn't anything obviously wrong with Zip, either, so she quickly put both bots back together. She'd been working with bots for her entire life, so it wasn't hard.

"You need more sleep," Zip admonished her as soon as he was put back together.

"Later."

"The mechanic hasn't called you yet. Sleep now."

He gently pushed her back towards her room, following her at a sedate pace until she got into her bedroom.

She fell back into her bed, hugging one of her pillows. She

didn't know what was going to

happen, but she didn't like it at all.

Mechanic's Call

Annaisha

Annaisha woke up when she heard buzzing coming from her glow pad. She accepted the call, projecting a hologram of her mechanic in the room.

"I can't fix them."

Her heart leapt.

"What do you mean?" He could fix everything.

"Whatever is wrong is beyond the capacity of my equipment to fix. You'll have to check with a specialist I know on Zhongguo."

"Zhongguo?" Annaisha rarely left her little planetoid in Riben's orbit.

"Zhongguo," he answered firmly. "I'm sending you the information now."

His hologram disappeared. Mere moments later, her glow pad lit up with information. She needed to contact someone named Sangui on Zhongguo.

She tapped the glow pad until she could call him.

A hologram of someone with a large nose wearing an elaborate hat immediately appeared.

"Assistant to his Royal Highness speaking."

Annaisha blinked.

"Sorry, I think this is the wrong number. I was looking for a bot mechanic." She lifted her hand to end the call, but then the hologram spoke.

"You've reached the right place."

She frowned. What could possibly be going on? Sangui was apparently a royal assistant. She didn't know why the mechanic had sent her in this direction. Sangui might be able to help, but she didn't know if she could afford it.

"I read the information that was sent over this morning. You must be Annaisha."

"I am."

"If you'd like, you can come to Zhongguo with some of your AI. We might have a solution to the dilemma that you're facing at the moment, but we need a defective bot and a working one to get a good grip of the situation. Can you do that?"

"Yes." Annaisha's heart sped up. Could Sangui be the answer?

"Then we'll purchase a ticket

for you on the next ship between Zhongguo and Riben."

"Thank you, sir." She bit her lip. "How much will it cost?"

"Something reasonable," he assured her. "I take a special interest in Riben robotics, and I am eager to diagnose what might be going wrong. Bye."

Then his hologram disappeared. Annaisha practically ran out of her room to find Zip, pulling him into her arms and twirling him around like a party bot. He tolerated the indignity, though he didn't have the capacity to dance.

"We're going to be fine," she said, hope blossoming like a new flower in her heart.

"Why?"

"There's somebody on Zhongguo who can fix us...the bots."

"You are not a bot."

No, she wasn't, but she felt

closer to her bots than most Ribenren.

"Our luck is turning." Her recreational business hadn't been that great this season, but as soon as she got her bots healed, she could be back in business.

She hurried back to her room to close the schedule for future visitors. She was leaving her planetoid, and she couldn't possibly look after any guests at the moment. Fortunately — or unfortunately, depending on how you looked at it — she didn't have any guests on her planetoid right now.

She skipped to her closet, a song in her heart. She would pack just her essentials and be ready for the transport spaceship to Zhongguo. She'd never been there, and it would be an interesting trip, no matter if they could actually fix her bots or not. She'd swing by the mechanic's workshop to pick up her bots, and then she'd leave most of them at home while she took Zip and one of the defective bots to Zhongguo.

Transport Spaceship

Annaisha

Annaisha tapped her feet while she waited to enter the spaceship. She had her ticket on her tablet, and she couldn't wait to get on this ship. She was fully packed, and most of her bots were resting at home. Zip was hovering at her side, lacking her impatience since he was, in a sense, eternal. He would live far longer than a creature of flesh and blood, as long as the virus that had taken out her dance bots didn't hit him.

She bit her lip and tried to cry in front of all the other passengers. Her entire livelihood was at stake here. If she couldn't fix her bots...she'd be totally lost. Her entire life had been dedicated to bots and the park. Without them, she had no idea who she was. She tried to keep it together in public, but it was a battle to keep her tears at bay.

Finally, someone was checking her ticket. She went inside of the spaceship. For some reason, she had a luxurious bunk. She wasn't precisely poor, not with the recreation park, but she wasn't wealthy enough to splash money around wantonly, either. She appreciated that whomever she'd spoken to on the phone — Sangui, she thought his name was — had made the effort to book her a nice suite.

It had a wall that was completely made of windows. As the spaceship launched off-planet, she stared out into space. She didn't often travel away, so she appreciated the opportunity to see new things. She could see slowly rotating nebulas as the ship passed them, and she could see beautiful vortexes behind them.

"The vortexes are beautiful,

aren't they?"

Annaisha turned to look at Zip. She could see the wonder on his little face. She knew in her heart that Zip felt things, maybe differently from humans, but he felt emotions all the same.

She felt herself getting tired. She'd been stressed out by all the craziness that had gone on with her bots, and she knew that she should get a little rest. Zip stayed at the window while she leaned back into her comfortable bunk

and waited to arrive in Zhongguo.

Docking

Annaisha

She woke up when the ship docked with a large thunk that shook her entire room.

"We're here," Zip told her.

"I know."

She gathered her things, her poor broken bot among them, and she went to the exit. She overheard a conversation from two girls who were standing in front of her. Their luggage was shiny; it looked like it had gold plating on the outside. What a crazy waste of money. Real gold corroded pretty easily, so putting it on the outside of luggage was the privilege of the extremely wealthy.

"Do you know that Zhongguo is where Zhanshi is from?"

Zhanshi? Who was that?

"No way!"

"Yeah! I don't know which

kingdom, but he's some kind of prince."

"Why would a prince want to fight?"

"I don't know…but he's pretty good at it."

"Stellar. I hope that we get to meet him."

"I would love that."

Annaisha didn't pay much attention to fighters, but she wondered if she would meet Prince Zhanshi while she was on

Zhongguo. Probably not. She was only here to fix her bots, and it didn't sound like he had anything to do with those.

Then again, Sangui had said that he was a royal assistant. It was possible but not probable, she decided.

The queue of people moved off of the ship, and she was grateful to be in the wide open space again. She didn't have claustrophobia, but she got nervous when she was in an enclosed space with a large number of people. She'd been distracted by staring out the window, and was glad that she didn't travel very much.

As she moved towards the transport station, she saw a sign with her name on it. She moved towards the sign while realizing that the man holding it was the same one who had spoken to her in the hologram.

Meeting Sangui

Annaisha

"Sangui?"

"You must be Annaisha. Welcome to Zhongguo. Do you have any more luggage?" He eyed her suitcase and her bots as if he was expecting three times the amount.

"Nope. This is it." Annaisha never over-packed. She knew how to give her clothes to a laundry bot after all, and there was no reason for anybody to have too many clothes.

"Well, you'll need to wear something...halfway decent...to the royal dinner tonight."

"Excuse me? Royal dinner? I came here for my bots."

"You've been invited to a royal dinner, my dear." She didn't like his smile. "It is a great honor, and it would be highly offensive if you declined."

Annaisha sighed. "Okay, then." She didn't know how to act around royals, but she supposed that she could put up with it for a few hours. It wouldn't kill her, though she definitely wasn't looking forward to it.

There was a levi-car waiting for them outside of the transport station, and she got into the car with her belongings. Sangui followed her inside. She didn't like being with him in such close

proximity, but there wasn't

anything she could do about it.

The levi-car took them a long

way. She stared out the windows,

taking in the landscape as it rolled

by. She had never been to

Zhongguo before. In some ways, it

resembled her home with a lot of

grass. In others, it really didn't. In

the distance, she could see the

crumbling blocks of a very old wall,

one that had been constructed

with a mixture of concrete that had stood the test of time. Even with a chemical analysis of the material, modern scientists couldn't figure out the composition. There were rumors that Zhongguoren remains made up part of the mixture, so nobody really wanted to use the exact same building materials. The countryside was both familiar and foreign.

When they got to a palace, the levi-car stopped. Annaisha gulped.

The palace was easily a hundred times larger than her own home. She was supposed to stay here?

"Are there any hotels or anything that I can go to?" She might be squeezed tight to afford it, especially with the repair bills coming soon, but she also knew that she'd sleep better at night if she didn't have to deal with the enormous palace.

"You are a royal guest. It would be rude."

Annaisha couldn't stop herself from sighing. It seemed that a lot of things that she wanted to do were considered rude.

"Do you have anything to wear?" Sangui's gaze was not flattering. He seemed slightly horrified by her clothes. Was Riben fashion way behind Zhongguo fashion? Was it too tight? Too revealing? Too loose? Too out-of-date?

"Um...maybe not." She had a

lot of clothes just like this, but she didn't really care.

"I'll have something sent to your room, then. Come this way."

He brought her through the palace until they came to an enormous staircase. As they climbed up it, she saw that there were many levels. Her thighs and calves ached by the time that they had gone up five flights of stairs.

"Rose or gold?"

"Excuse me?"

"Do you want a rose or gold room?"

She looked at Zip. Zip didn't respond at all, just staring straight back at her.

"Gold, I guess."

He unlocked a door and held it open for her. She tried not to freak out, but everything in the room was in shades of gold. The wallpaper was gold. The lamps were gold. Everything was gold-toned at the very least, and it was extremely shiny. It looked like the essence of luxury.

"This room will be yours for the duration of your stay on Zhongguo."

"This room is phenomenal." She worried that she seemed too boring, but she definitely didn't have a bedroom like this back on Riben.

He smirked a little, as if she were a country bumpkin. "I'll send a bot with your dinner clothing.

Settle in."

Settling In

Annaisha

She waited until he had walked out the door and closed it behind him to go into the bathroom. She really wanted to use the sonic shower. She wasn't dirty, really, but she didn't like the smell of that spaceship, and it seemed to have settled around her in a cloud of slightly gross stench.

When she got into the shower, she could see that the dials were totally weird. Back on Riben, she only had one dial: on and off. But on Zhongguo, they had a million buttons to press. None of the writing was in Standard.

She sighed as she wrestled with the controls, which looked more like the controls of a spaceship than the controls of a shower. Finally, she heard the sonic shower turn on.

She was immediately blasted with a wave of sound that sent her crashing backwards into the cold tile behind her. She fell on her bottom as another huge wave of sound hit her again.

Then it was over. She certainly felt just about the cleanest that she'd ever been in her entire life, but she didn't know if she wanted to repeat that experience. She wasn't too proud to ask about how to operate her shower; she'd just have to find a tactful way to bring it up that didn't start, "So I was naked in my shower when..."

She blushed when she thought about being so open with these Zhongguoren.

When she left her bathroom, she saw that a bot had come and gone. There was a very pretty dress on her bed. It was bright red with blue squiggles on it. If you had asked her yesterday if she'd ever wear a red dress with blue squiggles, she would have said no. But the dress itself was cut in a flattering way, and she shrugged it on.

Moving to the full-length mirror on one side of her room, she frowned and tugged the neckline up. It stubbornly slid straight back down, showing way too much chest. She took it off.

She rummaged around in her suitcase for a shirt so that she didn't scandalize the dinner guests. Surely the dress had been made for someone who was far taller than she was.

They had left her a small camisole as well, and she made a face as soon as she saw it. It was a very light pink, much more feminine than anything she normally wore, but it would have to do. It didn't fit with the blue squiggles at all when she put the pink camisole on top of the dress on the bed.

She supposed that if they had a fancy dress laid out for her, they'd want her to do something with the rest as well. She made a face at herself in the mirror. She'd never spent much time on her appearance, preferring instead to work on bots.

There was a machine in the corner which had a picture of a breathtakingly gorgeous woman on it. She pressed the big green button; the control panel was far simpler than the one for the shower.

Instantly, a cloud of powder was expelled, making her cough and choke.

"What the...?"

She never finished that sentence, because suddenly a robotic arm with a brush headed straight for her eye.

"Ah!" she screamed, backing away from the brush.

She felt a robotic arm push her

in a chair which seemingly materialized out of nowhere. She was terrified when, trying to back up, she hit the back of the chair and was kept in place between the robotic arm in front of her and the chair behind her.

She tried to move away from the brush, but it wouldn't let her.

Then it was touching her eyelid, and she realized that it was futile to resist the machine. It briskly touched both of her eyelids multiple times. She felt something happening to her lips, a smooth, cool layer of makeup being placed there. It finished everything by smoothing makeup over her cheeks.

The machine beeped finally, and the chair and the robotic arm vanished back inside.

She went to look in the mirror and was stunned to find that she was wearing what seemed like a libra of makeup on her face. She came close to the mirror. She'd never looked so good in her entire life.

She was afraid that putting the dress on would smudge the makeup, and she wasn't happy to go through that whole experience again, but she put the dress and camisole on anyway.

Her makeup was totally undisturbed. She put her finger to her jawline and tried to get some of the makeup off just as an experiment.

Nothing happened.

Somehow, the makeup that came out of that machine was totally smudge free. She didn't know how to take it off, but she'd deal with that later. Maybe it would stay on permanently? She admitted that she wouldn't mind being pretty without any effort.

She heard a knock at the door.

First Dinner

Annaisha

"Come in," she called. How lucky was it that someone had come just as she'd finished getting ready?

"It's nearly time for dinner," Sangui announced, coming into the room. His critical eye swept up and down, and he nodded once.

"You'll do."

Annaisha knew that she looked the prettiest she'd ever looked in her life, and Sangui's response was almost an insult.

"Come downstairs."

Annaisha was still wearing her own shoes, and she was grateful that Sangui hadn't thought to give her any kind of heels. She wasn't used to walking in them, and she wouldn't be able to go up or down the stairs safely in them, not without a very strong escort.

Sangui brought her downstairs again. By the time that she left the palace, her leg muscles would be huge.

As soon as she got down to the ground floor, she sniffed. She could smell the scent of roasted chicken, her favorite. She knew that the artificially grown meat that was from bovines was generally more favored, but she'd always been a fan of not-chicken.

The door to the dining hall was

open, and she went straight in.

As soon as Sangui and Annaisha passed through the door, a robotic voice announced Lord Sangui and Annaisha. The voice was so loud that it echoed throughout the hall. It seemed that it identified just about everyone who came in, though, because most of the people in the room didn't spare her a second glance.

Sangui brought her near the head of the table.

"You'll sit here, near the prince."

A tiny bubble of excitement grew in her stomach. Could he be the rumored champion? No, he couldn't be, she thought. If he was a famous champion, someone would say something.

She took a napkin and shook it out before placing it in her lap. She could smell all of the food, the wonderful aromas rising from the covered plates in front of her, but she also knew that she needed to respect Zhongguoren manners while she was on their planet. So she fidgeted a little bit waiting for the rest of their dinner companions to arrive.

She felt like the wind was knocked out of her when she saw a very tall man enter the room. His face was flawless, high cheekbones, deep dimples, flashing dark eyes. His skin was gold, a gold that glowed just a little bit.

She couldn't tell if it was from the lighting or an inner light.

She looked down at her own boring skin. She'd seen Intaran visitors, of course, so she wasn't a stranger to iridescent skin. Still, though, this man was one of the most attractive people she had ever seen in her life.

There was a tingle in her lower abdomen. She put a hand there, worried that something was going wrong.

"Hello." He sat next to her.

"I'm sorry, that seat is taken. It's supposed to be the prince's spot."

He gave her a killer smile with a flash of straight, white teeth.

"I'm the prince. Who are you?"

She felt her eyebrows shoot up. Her cheeks flushed with heat.

"Annaisha," she said softly.

"Excuse me?"

"Annaisha," she said a little more loudly.

"Nice to meet you."

"Nice to meet you, too. I never say no to a pretty girl sitting next to me at dinnertime." He gave her a wink that made her cheeks flush again.

Okay, he was very attractive, but she got major player vibes from him. She didn't have much experience with men, and she wouldn't start on the guy who would leave and break her heart. She didn't really have time while she was on Zhongguo to try out a relationship, anyway. She was only staying on this planet as long as it took to take care of her bots.

Then a dinner gong sounded. Everyone besides Annaisha got to his feet, and she quickly scrambled to mimic them.

From a door near the head of the table, a man who was obviously their king came through. Everyone was kneeling now, and Annaisha did the same a beat behind everyone else.

She realized now that she should've researched Zhongguoren manners before she ever landed. Then again, she never imagined that she'd be dining with a prince.

"Rise," the king commanded. Everyone got back into his seat.

The king flipped a small switch. The covers came off of their dinner plates.

Her mouth watered when she saw what was on her plate.

She was a big fan of Veronese melanzane alla parmigiana, and they had not one but two chicken breasts on top of the eggplant. The chicken breast was diced into bite-sized pieces.

She waited for the rest of the table to eat, and then she realized that everyone was staring at the king. He was unwrapping his utensils. They ate their food with chopsticks. Chopsticks made of wood.

She realized that everyone at the table was better than she was at using them. She used the cheater's method of crossing her chopsticks. Everyone else was using them properly, one chopstick kept firmly in place while the other chopstick was moved to pick up food.

Everyone was eating now, and she gasped when she realized that her glass was being filled with water from below. The

Zhongguoren had technology that she'd never seen before, and Riben wasn't exactly backwards.

She reached for her wine glass to pick up a little liquid courage. She might have been invited to the royal dinner, but she spent all of it being basically ignored. The king told raunchy jokes that she didn't quite understand, making all of the people sitting at the table laugh.

The only two people who weren't guffawing at the king's

jokes were the prince and

Annaisha. From the tightness

around his eyes she could tell that

he could understand the jokes, but

he was eating very quickly and

methodically. His dish was very

nearly empty.

She picked up her own pace.

She was far out of her depth in this

room and wanted to get back into

her bedroom, far away.

But she couldn't beat the

prince. The prince reached for the

cover, closing it so that the bots could pull the dirty plate away to be washed.

He bowed to his father, then he was gone. Annaisha quickly finished the rest of her dinner, and then she swiftly followed the prince out of the main doors.

Second Introductions

Annaisha

When she made her way to the stairs, she hummed to herself as she climbed all the way back up to her room.

She turned into the hallway to her room and then jumped a foot in the air. The prince was leaning on the wall right next to her door.

Her eyebrows shot up while

she put a hand on her heart to still its fast beat. "Can I help you, prince?"

"I'd like to introduce myself. I'm Zhanshi." He gave her that smile again. She imagined that a lot of women fell into bed with just that smile, but she was made of stronger stuff...or was just too inexperienced to experiment with the promise in his smile.

She smiled at him, grinning at his obvious attempt to dazzle her.

"You already know that I'm named Annaisha."

He nodded. His eyes were lingering on her curves for just a moment. She felt her skin heating up.

"I hope that your time with us is comfortable. Please contact me if there's anything that I can do to make you more comfortable."

"I will."

He bowed to her. She inclined her head, then the prince left her alone in the hallway, whistling the tune that she'd hummed to herself as she went up the stairs.

She was so embarrassed! She quickly went into her room, then checked on Zip, who was sorting through information after plugging himself into her terminal.

"Anything interesting going on?"

Zip was programmed to specifically find things that would interest her.

"Nothing."

She made sure that the door was locked before she got out of the borrowed dress. It was beautiful, true, but the cloth made her skin itch a little bit. It didn't fit quite right, even though it was definitely very lovely.

She lay down in just her camisole and undergarments on the huge bed which felt like it was made out of clouds.

The room around her was

made for a princess, not a recreational park owner who had a lot of sick bots. She didn't know why she was staying in the palace, but she supposed that she shouldn't complain, not when she was surrounded by more luxury than she'd ever seen in her life.

It was a compliment, she supposed. She didn't know why Sangui hadn't let her stay in a budget area, but she shouldn't look the gift horse in the mouth.

She rolled over and looked at herself in the mirror. She still had a full face of makeup. She went into the sonic shower again, this time not sure if it would fix everything.

Annaisha was able to brace herself against the blast, though it still hit her hard enough to make her stagger backwards.

When she was clean, she got out of the shower stall and ran towards her mirror. She touched her face. To her relief, the makeup was gone. It might be smudge-free, but it could be removed by the sonic shower. She looked at the machine in the corner of the room. She'd really like to take one home with her, but it was probably way too expensive for her. She sighed. She would do anything to make sure that her bots were okay, and today, it probably meant that she wouldn't be able to buy a makeup machine. Someday.

She unpacked her pajamas and slipped into them, comforted by their soft fabric. Once she was under the covers on her soft bed, Zip turned down the lights, and she closed her eyes. Her first day on Zhongguo had been a little scary, but she'd go see what could be done about her bots tomorrow.

Dressmaker

Annaisha

The next morning, Annaisha hit send on her comm mail. She hadn't seen Sangui since he put her in this room. Why hadn't he come back for her bot? She looked at Zip and his broken cousin. She wanted to get things fixed so that she could go back home. Sangui hadn't given her another call through her glow pad, and she was getting jittery about being penned up in this room.

"Zip, why won't Sangui answer me?"

"He's a royal assistant; he answers to them, not you. You're just a guest here."

"I guess that you're right."

Just then, her terminal had an elaborate invitation flash across the screen. It started out as an envelope, but it unfolded itself, letting multi-colored bubbles out of the envelope before the invitation was displayed.

Annaisha read it. It was from the prince. There was some kind of party tonight. He wanted her to come with him.

Her cheeks flushed as she thought about the handsome prince. Warmth kindled in the pit of her stomach when she thought about his dimples and killer smile.

Stop it, she told herself. It's

just a party invitation.

She went to look through her wardrobe. The dress that she'd been loaned the day before couldn't be worn again, which meant she didn't have anything to wear.

"Zip, could you look for some kind of dressmaker in the vicinity? Maybe they have one in the palace."

Zip plugged himself into the terminal and immediately beeped.

"There's a seamstress in the palace. They have a custom-made Fitter. You should visit her. She is on the third floor."

"Thanks, Zip."

Annaisha quickly got dressed into her own clothes since she had nothing else.

She went downstairs to find the seamstress. After walking around the third floor for ten minutes, she realized that she should have asked Zip for more specific instructions. In a building as big as the palace, the third floor was simply enormous. There weren't labels on the doors, just small little name cards.

She could've wept with frustration, but she gritted her teeth and kept going. Finally, she saw that one of the name cards had "seamstress" after it. She knocked on the door and then pushed it open. She hoped that the seamstress wouldn't think that she was too rude.

"Come in," the seamstress said a second after Annaisha's knock.

Annaisha walked inside of the room. There were racks upon racks of clothes of all colors and all kinds of patterns.

"Wow! I've never seen this many clothes in one place."

"I am a seamstress," the seamstress said with the smallest bit of reproof in her voice. "How can I help you?"

"I need a dress?" Annaisha hated herself for the question in her voice.

"That sounded like a question. Do you need a dress?"

"I got an invitation from Prince Zhanshi for a party tonight."

"I see." The seamstress looked at Annaisha, and Annaisha wanted to wipe the look of disdain off of the seamstress' face.

"Yes, I can understand why you're here."

"So you can help? How much will it cost?"

The seamstress waved her hand. "I'm employed by the king to ensure that everyone in this palace is properly clothed. Are you a guest?"

"I am."

"I thought as much, if the prince was inviting the likes of you to a party."

What did she mean by that?

"Step into my Fitter, please."

The seamstress motioned towards the corner of the room.

Annaisha walked towards it. The glass door opened automatically. There were little flutters of nervousness in Annaisha's stomach as the glass door closed.

She stood still as she was scanned.

She walked out and nearly shrieked when she saw a diagram of her naked body, and cringed with a little shame when she saw the softness of her stomach on the image.

"Let me see...you need something soon. Is the rest of your wardrobe like what you're wearing right now?"

"Yes."

"So I'll have to do something quick for tonight. Come back later for more clothes. We can't have a royal guest looking like...that."

Annaisha didn't know if she

liked the seamstress. She seemed to be brutally honest and very critical.

Meekly, Annaisha said, "Okay."

"Come back in a few hours. I can get the Fitter to print something out, but you can't go to a royal party in a simple pre-programmed outfit. You're top priority, and I'll have a drone contact you to bring you back for a fitting. I'll work on everyday clothing that's worthy of a princess."

"I'm not a princess, though."

The seamstress waved her hand. "When you live in the palace as a guest of the king, you might as well be."

Annaisha knew that it was sheer luck that she'd been invited here, but she bit her tongue. It wasn't the time to say anything, since the seamstress wasn't charging her anything specifically because she was a guest.

After Annaisha bowed to the seamstress she walked back to her room. She played a few games on her terminal to pass the time and keep her mind off of her bots' illness.

Butter

Annaisha

A few hours later, there was a heavy thud against her door. She hurried outside.

"Come to the seamstress," the droid outside told Annaisha.

Annaisha walked out and quickly followed the droid to the staircase. It seemed to dissemble itself and melt into the bannister before zipping downwards.

Annaisha had to walk down the way that flesh creatures had to: one step at a time.

She knew where she was going this time, so she went and opened the door to the seamstress' room.

"I have your dress for tonight ready already."

She looked at it. The skirt was a deep emerald, but the top was covered in...

"Are those bots?" she asked,

looking closely. How could the seamstress possibly know that she loved her AI?

"They are. The Fitter chose the pattern, heaven knows why. They are small enough to be unnoticeable unless someone comes very close to you and inspects you very carefully."

Annaisha wondered if the Fitter, this particular Fitter, had some brain scan capacity. While the prospect was exciting, it was also frightening. There were some

thoughts that should be private.

Her cheeks heated as she thought

about her secret thoughts about

Prince Zhanshi.

"Thank you very much."

"My job," she told Annaisha.

"Now leave. I have a lot more work

to do."

Annaisha bowed before she left

carrying the elaborate dress. It had

bots up top and the hem was

embroidered with some kind of

silvery thread. The square cut of the neckline was nothing like anything she owned. It was a lot more daring than anything that she really liked to wear, but she could wear a camisole under it just like her earlier dress.

When she got back to her room, she unzipped the dress and wiggled into it. To her dismay, it fit her as closely as a second skin. There wasn't any room for another shirt under the dress.

She realized now why the seamstress had asked her to come physically for the dress rather than sending it with the droid in the first place. But she didn't like the idea of going back and asking the seamstress to modify the dress now. She'd just have to wear it just as it was.

She looked at herself in the mirror. The cut of the neckline emphasized the curve of her breasts and the shadow between them. She admitted that the impact was nice, but it was far more revealing than anything that she'd buy. Ever.

She looked at her sick, powered down bot. She really wished that Sangui would get back to her about her sick bots, but Zip was right. When she was a guest, she couldn't pester them incessantly.

"Zip, do you think it fits?"

"It was made for you. Of course

it fits," Zip said pragmatically. "Do you think that their Fitter was defective?"

"No," she sighed. "I just would rather avoid this whole thing. I only came here for my bots, and I seem to be attending more social functions in a few days than I normally attend in an entire year."

"You're here for the bots. Don't forget it. You'd do anything to save us. If all of your party bots and dining bots die, you'll only have me...and Margaret."

"I feel bad about leaving her at home. She's every bit as well-made as you are."

"Margaret isn't your constant companion the way that I am. You're a little old for a nanny bot, anyway."

Could Annaisha hear pride and jealousy in Zip's voice? She quickly discarded the thought. AI might feel something, but they wouldn't feel jealousy.

Her glow pad chimed. She was supposed to be downstairs at the party.

She checked herself in the mirror, looking at the way that her dress fit her. It was flattering, true, but she'd leave the dress here once she returned home. There was no place in her life for dresses like this one.

She walked down the stairs to go into the dining hall. The entire ground floor was filled with nice smells. She could pick out soy sauce and cilantro, but she didn't know what else there was.

She saw Sangui conversing with the king, but he didn't even spare her a glance as she sat down in the seat that she had occupied before. Didn't he understand how urgent her situation was? Every day that her bots were out of commission, she was losing money. She could afford to take a little hit, but a big one would knock her life off kilter. If the virus spread throughout her entire recreational park, she'd lose her family of droids, the only place that had ever felt like home, and the livelihood that permitted her to spend all of her time with robots instead of flesh creatures.

The prince came into the room. She looked around. What differentiated tonight from the other night?

She could see that, unlike the

first night, there were actually females in the room this time. She realized with a slight shock that nearly everyone but her had been elderly and male...well, besides the prince.

She looked at him. The prince was definitely male. She admired the breadth of his shoulders, which were only accentuated by his royal uniform. She didn't know if he had to wear it every day or if he was wearing it just for the party, but it definitely made him look very good...good enough to eat.

Annaisha blushed when those thoughts went through her mind. She caught his eyes. He had been watching her watch him, which just made her blush more.

She looked at her plate, which was opening now. The king must have flipped the switch when she wasn't looking. Now they were having some kind of Oxitan dish.

"Canard à l'orange is one of my favorite dishes. How about you?" the prince asked.

"I can't say that I've eaten a lot of duck." Back home, when she was by herself, she ate a lot of quickly prepared ramen. It was the expensive kind, the sort with fresh meat that she would serve to her visitors. Still, noodles and soup were the quickest meal that she could get from her dining bots. She preferred to spend as little time as possible cooking, and they definitely helped her there.

She picked up her knife — no chopsticks today — and carefully cut her duck. She quickly realized that duck had a lot more bones than a chicken did, or maybe all the chicken that she ate was deboned.

She frowned. "Is this lab grown?"

The king must've come to a pause in his conversation, because he butted into theirs.

"Lab grown! We don't eat lab grown meat in royal palaces in Zhongguo, girl!"

Annaisha crossed her arms. She was deeply embarrassed by her faux pas.

"I'm sorry," she said tightly. "I didn't mean to offend anybody."

"No offense taken," the king said, still laughing at her. "But I'd no sooner see lab grown meat on this table than I'd see rat." He turned back to the other side.

Miserably picking at her duck, Annaisha thought about what he said. Her face turned green as she thought about eating living animals. On Riben, because there was a lack of grazing land for the animals, they only had lab grown meat. Yes, there was a lot of grass, but it was shocking how much grass animals needed to consume. She'd seen dairy cows grazing outside, so she knew that bovines could exist on Riben, but she also knew that the land area that was allotted to agriculture could not possibly sustain a large population. Butter, milk, and cheese were very expensive on Riben, because quite a bit of it had to be imported from off-planet.

She thought back to the day before, when she'd eaten melanzane alla parmigiana at the royal table. They casually ate cheese here, as if it weren't incredibly expensive. Either they were so rich that it didn't matter, or they could get it more cheaply than it was available on Riben.

Riben's government had trade protections in place which didn't really comply with the Intergalactic Federation's guidelines, but the IF hadn't yet smacked them or imposed any sanctions for their protectionist policies. Riben wanted to encourage local production of dairy products, so they offered subsidies for dairy farms while heavily taxing imports. Butter was one of the most expensive condiments on Riben; it was necessary for a lot of baked goods, so baked goods were also priced at a premium rate.

Annaisha looked at the table. There was a basket of small cookies on the table in the center.

"Can I eat those?"

"We normally wait for dessert...but why not?"

Annaisha reached out to eat one of the small cookies. She took a bite.

"This is a butter cookie!"

"Yes. My father is fond of them."

Annaisha didn't want to look like a poor bumpkin, so she didn't say that butter cookies on Riben were very rare. Not enough people had the money to buy them, since they required so much butter, and so they weren't produced very often.

Annaisha concentrated on cutting her duck. It required a lot of focus, because the bones were put together in a very strange way that Annaisha had never seen before.

Finally, the king left the dining hall, taking Sangui with him. Annaisha hadn't had a real chance to talk to the expert about her bots yet. She heaved a sigh of frustration.

"Lights," the prince said.

Annaisha turned to him, raising her eyebrows as the lights in the room totally shifted from normal-colored lights to rotating colored lights.

The table was sinking into the floor, which had two small metal doors that were open for it.

"Time to party," the prince shouted.

Annaisha abruptly realized that all the women in the room

were dressed in dresses like hers.

It really was a party.

What was she doing here? She wanted to get her bots healthy again, not stand around at some party where she knew basically nobody.

Important Business

Annaisha

Annaisha slipped out of the room quietly, leaving behind the party prince and his adoring fans. She knew that she didn't fit into this life...maybe in another universe she could be that kind of person.

Back in her room, she sat down at her terminal and sent

another comm mail to Sangui. She

didn't have very high hopes for an

answer

She peeled off the custom-

made dress and left it in a heap on

the floor. She was freezing cold

suddenly. She didn't want to be on

Zhongguo anymore. She wanted to

go home to her little recreation

park on the planetoid. Yes, she

wouldn't be able to find anybody to

fix her bots there, but she'd just do

it herself.

She pressed her lips firmly together and sniffed hard when tears threatened. Annaisha felt hopeless, because whatever was going on with her robots was definitely beyond her abilities...but she hadn't found the help that she needed on Zhongguo. At this point, she felt as if fixing her bots was impossible.

She packed what little she'd brought. Zip helped her bring the spare, broken bot by carrying it himself. She took the bots downstairs.

Outside of the palace, she realized that she didn't have the slightest idea of how to get to the space docks.

"Zip, can you figure out how to get us back to the docks and onto a spaceship that will take us home?"

\Zip thought about her request.

"We'll need a levi-car," Zip said

finally. "There are no public transportation options near the palace as a security precaution."

It figured. She'd had terrible luck since she'd arrived on Zhongguo.

"Can you hail one please?"

"Yes." She could hear Zip's gears whirring.

"Done."

"Thank you, Zip."

She sat on her suitcase while she waited for the levi-car to get to her. Her trip to Zhongguo had been somewhat expensive and hadn't helped her at all.

She would not cry. She wouldn't.

Finally, the levi-car arrived. After she climbed into it, Zip brought the other bot and her suitcase. They sat in the levi-car in total silence. Annaisha was a breath away from crying, but she needed to keep it together. She could cry in partial privacy inside of the car, but she didn't want everyone at the space docks knowing that she was a big baby.

She bit her lip to keep her frustration inside until they got to the docks.

When the levi-car slowed its motion, she got out and carried her luggage, Zip and the other bot following behind. She walked towards the dock master.

"Hello!" she said with substantially more cheerfulness

than she really felt. "Can I buy passage on one of the commercial ships?"

"Certainly!" he told her. His voice was big and deep. He sounded like the epitome of competence. "Let me just have your credit pass. It can identify you in the system."

"Sure." She handed him her credit pass.

He plugged it into his terminal. Both of them waited for it to be authorized.

DENIED flashed across the screen in big red letters.

"It can't be denied...I might not be rich, but I'm not out of money."

"Do you have another credit pass with you?"

With a sinking heart, Annaisha said, "No."

"I'm sorry, miss. I can't help you."

"But I..."

Zip touched her arm gently.

She turned to see the look on his face. He told her without words that arguing wasn't worth it.

"Thank you for your time," Annaisha said. It wasn't the dock master's fault that her credit pass wasn't working.

"I'm sorry...please come back when you've fixed it."

"I will."

Annaisha went back to the levi-car, which was still exactly where she left it. Why hadn't it moved on? Had it not been called by someone else? Or had the levi-car known that she'd be denied?

If that was the case, then how could she possibly have paid for the levi-car? Zip had all of her financial information, of course, and she'd paid for the levi-car in advance. Being denied at the space dock was very, very strange.

The levi-car brought her straight back to the palace. Something was definitely weird about the levi-car; the route that it had taken had somehow been pre-programmed to take her places without being told.

"Thank you," she told the levi-car. Someone else would've been surprised by the little light display that the levi-car did when she got out, but she knew better than anyone on this planet that AI had feelings.

She dragged her suitcase into the palace and headed for her

room, Zip behind her. She came into her suite and let Zip go first; Zip dumped the other robot unceremoniously on the ground before plugging himself into a power outlet. She felt guilty for not even considering how draining the whole thing had been for Zip.

"Ahem."

Interceding

Zhanshi

Zhanshi stopped by Annaisha's room before he went to bed. She'd left before the party started.

He was legendary for the parties that he threw, parties that his father loved. They fit in with the playboy prince persona. To be truthful, he'd tired of the parties long ago, but he had to keep up with his public image. The parties were something to do at night, anyway.

He saw that the door was open and her bot was plugging itself into the wall. He cleared his throat and watched her whirl around to face him.

"What are you doing here?"

He answered her question with a question. "Why do you have a suitcase in your hand? Why are you leaving so soon?"

He watched as a single tear spilled from the corner of her eye. She wiped it away with the back of her hand.

"I just...I came here so that I could fix my bots, but it seems as if I'll never get them fixed." Tears were falling faster now. "Sangui seems very busy, and I really have to go home...but they wouldn't let me get onto a spaceship."

Zhanshi reached down to take the handle of her suitcase. He put an arm around her shoulders and noticed how sweet she smelled, almost like a flower. Perfume tended to be heavier and artificial, but he thought that the light floral smell might just be Annaisha's natural essence.

He walked into her bedroom, which smelled like her even after her short stay in it.

"I'm sure that Sangui can slot you into his schedule."

"But he can't. I've sent comm

mails...and he never replies."

"I'll talk to him about it. Let me take a shot, okay?"

Her tears dried. "If you think you can help."

"I know I can," Zhanshi said, giving her a lopsided grin. "Let me take care of it."

She was smiling now, and her smile made Zhanshi's heart clench.

"Why not?"

Seeing that her tears were done falling, he said, "I'll go now.

Bye."

Zhanshi walked out of her room while fighting the urge to whistle. The pretty Ribenren was definitely focused on her bots and not even remotely interested in the lifestyle that he had to pretend to lead. She was definitely a breath of fresh air when he was surrounded by groupies who wanted to get naked with a prince, especially a prince who had a long history of winning fights and quadrant-wide fame.

Zhanshi walked to Sangui's quarters, which were on the floor below his father's. Sangui was theoretically on call at any time of the day or night. Zhanshi had never liked Sangui, his father's right hand, but he didn't know if that was because of his position or because of the man himself.

He knocked on Sangui's door.

"A moment."

Zhanshi counted to thirty

before the door opened.

"Prince Zhanshi." Zhanshi could hear in Sangui's voice that he was startled to find the prince at his door. "How can I help you?"

Zhanshi pushed past Sangui to get inside of his space. He noted that the outer room was cluttered with detritus associated with bots.

"I heard that Annaisha needed some help with her bots."

"I'm more than happy to help," Sangui said, "but I'm afraid I'm swamped with repairs at the moment. I can't possibly help right now. Perhaps there will be an opening in the schedule when your father returns."

"What? Where did he go?"

"He's off-planet at the moment...you didn't know?"

"No."

"Well, he's away on important business."

"Annaisha said that she's been sending you comm mail that you're not responding to."

Instantly, Sangui glanced at the terminal in the corner. Zhanshi looked, too, and he could see the unread messages from Annaisha.

"I haven't had a chance to reply to them." He coughed. "But I'm sure that I'll get to them soon. I'm busy at the moment, Your Highness, so if you wouldn't mind."

Zhanshi found himself being forced to walk towards the door as Sangui got inappropriately close to him.

"Goodnight, Your Highness."

Zhanshi realized that he was in the corridor. The door to Sangui's suite slid shut between them.

Well! What a very strange visit. Sangui, while not a complete sycophant, didn't tend to do anything that would anger the royal heir, at least not directly. He should've complied with Zhanshi's request. The mere fact that he hadn't meant that his father, the king, was up to something. Sangui obviously knew what was going on. Why hadn't Annaisha been able to get on a spaceship to take her home?

He had a bad feeling in his gut about his father's intentions for Annaisha. He needed to walk back to her room to talk to her.

Library

Annaisha

Annaisha heard a knock at her door.

"Can I come in?"

"Please do." Annaisha hurried to the door and opened it just as he did, ending up toe to toe with the handsome prince. He was mid-step, bringing him close enough for her to feel his body heat. She felt a melting sensation in the pit of her stomach.

"Oh, I'm so sorry," Annaisha said, stumbling backwards. Her cheeks grew hot as she thought about how ungraceful she was, especially in comparison to the athletic prince.

"No problem. I'm the one who should be apologizing. I thought that it would be simple to get the problem with your bots fixed, but Sangui seems quite preoccupied at the moment."

Annaisha sat on her bed. "So what does that mean?"

"No worries. I have a way with code, and we've got the best books in the galaxy. If you've got this much money, you might as well buy what you want. I have a special interest in bots, myself, although my father discouraged it. He thinks that it's not royal to tinker with robots, but my mother's family owned a lot of bot factories. I built my first one when I was about two."

"Two? That's really young. I couldn't read instructions at two."

"My mom helped, of course. The bot that I made was color-coded, anyway. It came with step-by-step instructions with pictures."

"Like building blocks?"

"Exactly." He winked at her. Another surge of heat filled her, but it didn't go to her cheeks. It went straight to her core. It was like the bottom half of her body was melting.

"So what do you say? Do you want to go to the library?"

"Yes."

Annaisha hadn't ever been in a library before, not in an age when every book that anybody would want was digitized and easily available on the Intergalactic Federation's Net. Still, it would be an interesting experience.

"Let's go, then."

Annaisha followed Zhanshi out
to the corridor. He brought her
down a few flights of stairs before
they were at a door that smelled
like vanilla.

"Is this a kitchen?"

"No," he told her as he pushed
open the door. "It's the library."

When the doors opened,
Annaisha's first impression was
one of vast space. The ceilings were
high. She could see tracks for
small bots to retrieve books. It

wasn't as efficient as digitized versions, of course, but she had to admit that the smell was nicer.

"Let me take you to our collection of information on bots."

Zhanshi walked through the library until he turned a quick right through a few shelves.

"Here we are."

Annaisha felt her mouth open as she looked at the sheer quantity of books there. She easily had a few hundred books about bots, but her collection could not rival Zhanshi's.

There were easily thousands of books there, possibly over ten thousand.

"Why would you have this many books?"

"I told you...I take an interest in bots."

Annaisha kept her mouth shut then, although she wondered if having such a huge library of physical books — playthings and

status symbols for the wealthy —
was really a wise idea.

Zhanshi was keying information into a small terminal now. Annaisha watched as several small bots zoomed around.

"I picked up some of the comprehensive diagnostic books."

"Could we just run a search?"

"Where's the fun in that?" Zhanshi flashed his dimples at her. "Besides, I want to spend time with you."

Annaisha had no idea what to say to that. She wasn't really sure how to take it. She had been on her own for a long time, and she certainly never bothered to make time for any real romance.

The timing was awful. She would leave Zhongguo as soon as she got the credit situation sorted out or when Sangui finally answered her comm mail and fixed her bots. She wouldn't be around for that long, so she should stay away from Zhanshi.

Records Room

Zhanshi

A few hours later, their search had been completely fruitless. Zhanshi had learned more than he ever wanted to know about bot viruses, but he still was empty handed.

"I'm sorry that I've brought you here for nothing."

"It's okay...at least we tried."

"There's just one more place to go."

"Oh?"

"I'm not supposed to go there."

"Where?"

"The records room."

"But there's more information there?"

"Yes. Go back to your room. I'm going to sneak in."

"Will you be okay?"

"Of course." Zhanshi winked. "Nothing to it." Sure, he didn't have any kind of authorization to go into the records room, but what was the point of being royal if he couldn't bend the rules a little bit?

"I'll swing by your room in an hour."

"Okay, I'll see you then."

Annaisha walked away. Zhanshi admired the sway of her hips as she did, then he shook himself as he refocused on his mission. He needed to get into the records room.

He shouldn't have a pass code at all, but a very inebriated pretty lady had told him how to get in during his last party. She was one of the records keepers, the holders of the keys to a very tightly controlled vault. He was her prince, after all...it wasn't as if he'd betray the kingdom and misuse the information.

He went to the back corridors, staying away from everywhere that he knew had a surveillance camera. He'd missed his calling; he would've liked to be some kind of assassin or spy. Instead, he was stuck with being a boring prince trapped in a life he hadn't chosen.

He checked the area around the records room, but it was empty. Entering the room, he entered the pass code, and then sat down at a terminal connected to the kingdom's deepest secrets, a vault of information kept in darkness.

Flexing his fingers, he got ready to work. Then he started tapping around and searching for documents that had to do with Annaisha's robots.

A search on Annaisha's name brought up her bots and her interaction with Sangui, including her repeated comm mails asking for help. It showed that she had been sent from Riben without any knowledge of what the Zhongguoren wanted from her.

Zhanshi gasped as he saw a file labeled "marriage license". He opened it. Inside, there was a marriage license application with his name on it...and Annaisha was listed there, too. There was a copy of the deed to her recreation park planetoid and a comm mail screen shot of a local paper smith and code-changer's cards.

Annaisha had to see this. He had no idea why his father wanted her planetoid, but he could easily guess that it wasn't so that his father could own a recreation park.

He pulled a data stick out of his pocket so that he could save the data. It took no time at all, which made him wonder just how powerful the record room's computers were. They were twice as fast as his personal computers.

Zhanshi walked out of the room and bounced off of one of the members of the king's guard with Sangui in tow. Only his quick reflexes saved him from sprawling on the ground; he stood his ground.

Sangui said, "Your Highness, what were you doing in the records room?" He made a sound with his tongue that Zhanshi found incredibly annoying. Sangui had no right to tell him what to do.

Two of the guards went to either side of him, getting too close to him. Zhanshi flexed his fists and adjusted his stance, his heart rate rising. Yes, the king's guard was armed, but he was a fighting champion. If he couldn't take on a squad of the king's guard, then he was really out of practice.

"Zhanshi?"

Zhanshi, Sangui, and the members of the king's guard all looked to see Annaisha in the hallway.

"I was looking for you. You and Zip left me alone. Have you seen him?"

Sangui looked at the guards and shook his head. Instantly, the two that were about to grab Zhanshi stepped back.

"Your father will hear about this."

Zhanshi didn't like the tone of Sangui's voice at all. What had his father ordered Sangui to do?

Abducted

Annaisha

"Zhanshi, what's going on? Why are your eyebrows furrowed?"

"Time is of the essence. We have to get moving."

"What?"

"Let's go to your room."

Annaisha basically had to run to keep up with Zhanshi's longer legs as he quickly walked back to her room, quickly bringing her through multiple corridors. She was glad that she was with him, because if she tried to get back to her room at this speed, she'd get lost. She was out of breath by the time that they got back to her room. Zip was standing right there in the corner, charging as if he'd never disappeared. She needed to ask him where he'd gone without telling her, but Zhanshi was pushing her towards her wardrobe.

"Pack now."

"But I...I'm packed, but I'm all sweaty from that run you just made me do."

"Shower as quickly as you can. Let's go."

"Okay, then." Annaisha walked into the sonic shower, drawing up the hem of her dress to bring it over her head. Her face flushed as she realized that Zhanshi could see through her open door; their eyes met. She was used to being on her own, with just her bots around. He gave her a crooked smile that told her that he liked what he saw, open appreciation in his eyes before he turned away. Still red-faced, she went to close the door before she hopped into the shower.

She turned it on quickly and used the buttons that she knew really worked to finish as quickly as she could. She put her dress back on. It was sweaty, but it would have to do. She didn't really have another choice.

"I'm ready."

Zhanshi had her suitcase in his hand. As she walked out of the room, he lunged forward and put an arm around her waist, sending warm tingles straight into her stomach.

"Come on."

She followed him down and out of the palace. They got into a small vehicle that was built for just two people. Her suitcase was strapped to the back of the vehicle while she sat in the back seat with her legs around the driver's seat. Zhanshi strapped into place and started the engine, roaring to life.

Annaisha could feel the vibrations of the engine shake the whole vehicle. It was almost like the recreational motorcycles that she had at her park, but it was fully enclosed like a levi-car. It also touched the ground, so it was substantially cheaper than a levi-car. Annaisha made a mental note to look into getting these vehicles for her park.

Then Zhanshi was forcing the vehicle to perform at its top speed. Annaisha didn't know where they were going, but the roar of the engine would drown her out if she tried to ask Zhanshi, so she kept quiet.

She couldn't see that well past Zhanshi's seat, but she could catch tiny glimpses of their route.

"Why are we at the space docks?"

"We're getting into a ship. They wouldn't let you buy passage on a commercial flight, so we're going to have to take matters into our own hands."

"Wait, what? No! I can't leave Zip by himself on Zhongguo."

The vehicle came to a complete stop. The doors opened, and Zhanshi pulled Annaisha out of it with a hand around her wrist. She watched as the doors closed and the car-motorcycle drove itself back in the direction from which they'd come.

"Why is it leaving us here? I'm not leaving Zhongguo without Zip."

Zhanshi's hand was still on Annaisha's arm, and he quickly pulled her over his shoulder. She hit her fists against his back, but he didn't seem to feel it at all. He ran quickly as if she didn't weight anything. His shoulders were easily twice the width of hers, making her feel very small when draped over his shoulder like this. It was a long way to the ground.

"We're getting onto my personal ship."

"No! You can't make me come with you! I need my bot!" Annaisha drew in a big breath so that she could shout for help.

But before she could, Zhanshi darted inside of a nearby ship and closed the outer door.

"You can scream now, if you want. The ship is soundproofed." He slipped her off of his shoulder and put her on her feet.

"Where are you taking me?" She looked at the door's control panel, which was even more complicated than her shower. She pressed a button that made an alarm go off. She covered her ears with her hands while Zhanshi walked over and turned the alarm off.

"I'm taking you back to your planetoid. I know what's going on now, and we need to get back as soon as possible if we want to prevent your worst nightmare."

Leaving

Annaisha

"What's that smell?" She could smell soy sauce and the scent of meat.

"I sent Zip ahead with my things while you were in the shower. He told me that he'd cook something for us."

Annaisha felt some of her worry melt away.

"Zip is already here?"

"He is."

She felt silly for throwing a tantrum about leaving Zip behind, but how was she supposed to know that Zip had been sent ahead? It wasn't as if Zhanshi had deigned to tell her what was going on.

"Strap yourself in. We're about to leave. I have special clearance to automatically get preference for take-off, and I don't think that my father has noticed what I'm doing yet."

"I don't even know what you're doing yet, and I'm here with you. Why did you take me to your ship? Stealing me without explaining anything is unacceptable."

"We don't have time for hysterics. We'll talk once we've gotten off of Zhongguo. Strap yourself in." He touched the control panel and made the ship move forward quickly in a way that almost made her fall. He still

wasn't answering her questions.

However, Zip's presence and the

prospect of some food made her

content to play along with

Zhanshi's unexplained plan. She

grabbed a seat before she could

embarrass herself by falling in the

moving spaceship and fastened a

harness around herself. She could

feel herself sinking into the gel

lining of the seat as the spaceship

gained velocity and launched into

space, flying past other ships.

Once they were clear of Zhongguo's atmosphere, the prince hit a big blue button.

"I put the ship on autopilot. I've set the coordinates so that we'll end up on your planetoid. I can show you what I found, if you like."

"Yes, please."

He pulled a data stick out of his pocket and plugged it into the control panel. Instantly, the view of space with stars and nebulae around them was replaced by gigantic versions of files.

"My father already arranged for a marriage license application to be written out. You can also see a sale certificate for your planetoid that already has your signature."

"But I haven't signed anything. I didn't sell my home."

Annaisha tried to do the math and came up short. She would never sign away her heritage. Why would there already be a signed sale certificate?

"My father is definitely after your planetoid. It's strategically important for trade; in some ways, it's underutilized as a recreational park. He only thinks about money. I'm sure that's where he's gone. His team probably found a way past your existing security and alerted him that they should go before you noticed. They figured out a way to keep you on Zhongguo to prevent you from coming back and ruining their plans."

Shoulders sagging, Annaisha bit her lip to stop herself from crying. She could hear the ring of truth in his voice; it made sense in a twisted way.

"Do you want me to turn the ship back so that we can go back to Zhongguo?"

Annaisha shook her head.

"No. I need to save my home." Her voice cracked, impossible to stop on the last word.

Zhanshi let the silence rest between them for a moment before saying, "Whatever Zip cooked smells really good. Let's go see what he made for us, okay?"

Annaisha wiped away a tear that leaked out of her eyes.

"Okay."

Teppanyaki

Annaisha

The two of them went to the galley of the ship.

"Stars! Zip made some of my favorite foods."

"He had the right stuff and the right equipment, Annaisha." Zip's face was calm, but Annaisha knew Zip better than she knew herself. He definitely approved of Prince

Zhanshi's handling of his ship. At this point, Zip would've connected to the mainframe of the ship. She smiled, since Zhanshi was beloved by his AI. It was easier to measure people by the way that they treated those below them than the people that were above them. AI was often considered inanimate, without any kind of feelings, and it was easy for people to believe that AI was just a tool. She knew better, of course, but she had never been successful in convincing other people to understand her point of view, so she'd stopped trying.

Zip had beautifully arranged their food on two different plates.

"What's all this?"

"Takoyaki and okonomiyaki," Zip told Prince Zhanshi, pointing at each one in turn. "Annaisha is fond of eating lab-grown octopus."

Prince Zhanshi raised his eyebrow. "Okonomiyaki looks like nokdujeon from Cria or banh xeo from Dalat. I haven't eaten lab-grown octopus before, but I'm certainly willing to try."

Annaisha approved of his open attitude. They picked up their plates and the chopsticks that Zip had already laid out for them.

Prince Zhanshi took his first bite of takoyaki and swallowed. "Wow, this is so good."

"You can see why they are my favorites, right?"

"This takoyaki is one of the

best things that I've ever eaten in my whole life. Crunchy, savory, smooth... Zip, where did you learn to cook like this?"

"The dining bots at home," Zip said.

Reminded of her home, Annaisha felt a lump in her throat that prevented her from eating any more. She put her plate down and hugged herself. If Zhanshi's father was successful, she'd lose her home.

Where would she go? For some reason, Zhanshi's father wanted Annaisha to marry Zhanshi. He was nice, but she couldn't imagine living permanently on Zhongguo. It was so foreign, and she was used to a lot more solitude than she got while living in the palace.

"Well, I'll have to see if you can send it to my bots. I really like takoyaki."

"It would be my pleasure."

Annaisha was happy that Zip

was being helpful to Zhanshi. Sometimes he could be a little less than courteous. She realized that she'd been rude to Prince Zhanshi by not acknowledging the help that he'd given her. They'd barely met, but he was willing to work against his father.

"Thank you for figuring all this out and helping me," Annaisha said. It was inadequate, totally inadequate, but she didn't know what else to say.

"My pleasure," he said, echoing Zip's reply.

Annaisha and Zhanshi quickly finished off the food that Zip had cooked for them. As they were eating their final bites, an alarm went off. It was a different pitch than the one that Annaisha had accidentally set off when she tried to open the door.

"I better go see what's going on." Zhanshi put his plate into a disposal slot and walked steadily back towards the control room.

Annaisha admired his total cool

even as the ship alerted them that

something was wrong.

Asteroid Belt

Annaisha

"You'll want to strap yourself in, Annaisha. You, too, Zip."

Annaisha walked into the main area. The ship did a sudden swerve that made her land on her butt. She would have a bruise there later.

"What's — ?"

She never finished that

sentence, because the ship tilted in the other direction quickly.

Zip was way faster than she was and had already linked himself to a chain on the wall. Annaisha crawled to the seat that she had used before, since she wasn't too sure about walking while the ship was like this.

"Hurry. We're in the middle of an asteroid belt."

Annaisha stood for long enough to get into the seat and

strap herself in. A millisecond after she clicked the last buckle of her harness, she felt Zhanshi take the ship in a huge loop.

"Woo!" he shouted, his hands over his head. He was clearly loving this, but Annaisha thought that she might see her takoyaki a second time. She put a hand over her mouth, determined not to spew in front of Zhanshi. It would be too embarrassing to barf in front of the handsome prince.

"Gonna cloak us at the moment." He flipped a switch. Annaisha could hear a very faint hum as the cloaking mechanism kicked in.

His easy mastery of the spaceship dazzled Annaisha. She didn't want to distract him by asking questions — now they were zooming around another curve — but she wondered why someone with his flight skills wasn't already in the quadrant's air force. He'd be a shoe-in with the flight skills he had.

Warmth blossomed in her heart when she thought about Prince Zhanshi taking the time to help her. He could be doing anything else, really, but he decided to be with her.

Finally, they reached the end of the belt. He pushed the same big button that he'd pushed before to set the ship on autopilot. Annaisha wasn't sure if she saw just the tiniest bit of regret in his eyes; she guessed that he'd really loved the adventure of navigating the spaceship through the asteroid belt.

"I should show you the rest of the ship," he said. "It's been a wild ride so far, even though you've barely been inside. Come on. Zip, you keep an eye on the ship, okay?"

"Yes, Your Highness," Zip replied, unlinking himself from the chain and plugging himself into the mainframe. "I will keep watch."

"Thanks, Zip!" Prince Zhanshi grabbed Annaisha's arm and linked it with his. Her skin flushed at the contact.

"My ship isn't that big, but it's really supposed to be just for me. I have two small capsule bunks and a kitchen, and that's pretty much it. Through the engine room, I have a recreational center with virtual reality via a holo-deck, but I don't spend much time there. The ship would tell me if anything was really wrong, of course, but I'd rather not take a chance, generally. Would you like to try out my holo-deck? It deserves a lot more use considering how many credits it cost."

"I'd love to check out your holo-deck. I have some sim rooms, but I don't think I've tried a holo-deck before."

"Come on."

Holo-Deck

Zhanshi

Zhanshi fiddled with the terminal of the holo-deck. He didn't want to look like an idiot in front of Annaisha, but he wasn't all that familiar with the controls. He hoped that he looked competent. She'd been really impressed by his steering skills, but he wanted to show her a different side of himself.

"Do you like beaches?"

"Yes."

"Here, put on these goggles."

Annaisha picked up the goggles that he handed to her and strapped them on.

"The sand is blue!"

"Yeah." Zhanshi put on his own VR goggles and saw that Annaisha was kneeling and touching the sand.

"I've never seen sand like this

before."

"I'm sorry that I haven't taken you around Zhongguo."

"It's really okay. I didn't come as a tourist."

"There are a lot more things that you should've seen while you stayed with us. I don't feel like a very good host."

"It's okay," Annaisha soothed. "When do you think that we'll land on my planetoid, Xenkaku?"

"We aren't going straight there.

We're going somewhere else."

Annaisha got to her feet inside of the VR world. "Where?"

"It's a surprise."

Zhanshi switched the setting to a small volcanic island. They watched as the lava flowed down from the active volcano and hit the water, causing an explosion. There were volcanoes on Riben, of course, but Annaisha had never been so close to an active volcano, even through virtual reality.

As she spent more time playing around with Zhanshi, Annaisha felt a lot more comfortable with him. He liked to have fun, it was true, but he'd also taken care of her as best he could. She recognized that one reason why they were going through a virtual version of Zhongguo was to distract her from brooding about things that they couldn't control. They were going to try to save her home, and while she was in the ship, she couldn't do much.

While they were still watching the lava flow, the ship sent an alert. It wasn't as urgent as the asteroid belt, but Zhanshi had to go back.

"You can stay here and play some more. All you have to do is ask it to show you something else."

"I'm fine," Annaisha said. "It's fun, but I'm really tired all of a sudden."

"I've got two capsules. If you

just want to sleep, go grab one of them. I'll go check on the ship."

Annaisha yawned and covered her mouth with her hand.

"I'll go rest." She walked in the direction that Zhanshi pointed and found two small capsules. She climbed inside of one of them and was out like a light.

Academy Station

Annaisha

Annaisha woke up when the ship docked. She scrambled out of the capsule bed.

"Where are we?'

"One of the Academy stations."

"Why are we at a school?"

He winked at her. "We're here to pick up a friend."

The three of them walked off of

the ship and were immediately surrounded by guards.

Zip said, "Or a prison sentence."

"Who are you?"

"Lupo Lawless," Zhanshi said.

None of the guards moved an inch.

"I'm here to see Meizhen. Just tell her that Lupo is here. She can clear everything up."

Annaisha rubbed the back of her neck. Was Meizhen his

girlfriend...or one of them? She thought that there might be a spark between them, but now she wasn't sure. He hadn't made a move on her yet.

"We'll check with her. Stay right where you are."

Annaisha, Zhanshi, and Zip stayed next to their spaceship as the guards moved around, trying to confirm their identity and their right to be docked at the Academy station. After a few minutes, one of the guards came to them and said grudgingly, "You're free to go. Head into the heart of the station. Meizhen will meet you there."

The three of them walked past the guards and towards the center of the station. When they got there, Meizhen was standing right there. She was wearing an iridescent black gown that was one of the prettiest dresses that Annaisha had ever seen. Her hair was up in an elegant twist, something that

ALIEN CHAMPION'S BRIDE

Annaisha didn't understand how to do, and it was secured with several black pearl-tipped pins. To finish off her ensemble, she wore a black pearl necklace and bracelet.

"Zhanshi! What a pleasure to see you." She kissed his cheek. "And who is this?"

"Annaisha, I'd like you to meet one of my oldest friends, Meizhen."

Annaisha watched Meizhen's eyes flick up and down. Then she gave her a warm smile, and

Annaisha breathed a quiet sigh of relief. Meizhen wasn't competition.

"Let's go into my office," Meizhen suggested. "We won't be disturbed there."

They all moved into her office. When Zip closed the door, Meizhen spoke while they got settled in her chairs.

"So what's going on?"

"Here's the deal. I thought something fishy was going on, so I went and investigated it. I have some strange documents on this data stick."

"Strange how?"

"A marriage license."

Meizhen's eyebrows shot up. "I thought that you didn't want to marry, no matter how many women your dad pushed at you."

"I didn't, but he might just fake a marriage and be done with it."

"To whom?"

"Annaisha."

Meizhen switched her attention

to Annaisha.

"And what else?"

"We think that my dad is making a power play to get Annaisha's planetoid, Xenkaku. We have the data stick with some of the documents. Can you help?"

"Nothing has changed. I'm still the best hacker in the sector." She grinned at Zhanshi.

"Galaxy," he corrected.

Her eyes lit up. "I'd love a little bit of a challenge. Okay, here's what we'll do. You can stay here at the station with some passes while I dig into whatever is going on and doctor some leave papers. I'll meet up with you guys later." She tapped a keyboard that Annaisha hadn't noticed before. Some paper tickets spat out.

"Bye." Zhanshi was already on his feet with the passes in his hand. They were out the door when Zhanshi asked, "How does a space bar sound to you?"

Did he even have to ask?

"Lead the way."

Space Bar

Annaisha

Four hours later, Annaisha's beer was warm. She'd kept the same bottle in her hand since they'd arrived in the space bar, and she wasn't much of a drinker.

She watched as Meizhen and Zhanshi whispered to each other, which made Annaisha feel awkward. She felt like a third wheel.

She found herself yawning, her eyelids growing heavy. It was late. She didn't know what time it was, but her body definitely thought that it was night.

"Excuse me," she told them. "I'm going to go to rest."

The prince lifted a single finger. "Hold on."

"I needed to go anyway," Meizhen said. "I've got some code that I really have to finish now.

Bye. Don't drink too much."

Meizhen walked away from their table.

Zhanshi turned to her at once. "Do you want to dance?"

Annaisha didn't want to dance. She wanted to go to sleep. She suppressed another yawn.

"I'm not much of a dancer," she warned him.

"Maybe you've never had the right partner." He gave her a grin and took her hand. For some reason, she let him.

She realized that the dance floor wasn't like anything that she'd seen before. For one thing, it was spring-loaded. For another, there were lights that showed up to signal where to place your step.

"Just follow the lights," Zhanshi whispered in her ear as he pulled her close. Her body was plastered against his. She tried to pay attention to the dance steps, but it was hard when she was so close to Zhanshi. When she was this close, she could smell his masculine scent. She could feel his heartbeat. She liked the way that his arms were holding her tightly, creating a little warm glow in the pit of her stomach.

When she looked up at him instead of the floor, she gasped because his face was so close to hers, just a breath away.

"Tell me now: yes or no?" She could feel the hardness of his erection pressed against her stomach. Considering how little alcohol she'd had, it was strange that she felt so lightheaded.

"Yes."

Then Zhanshi was pulling them off of the dance floor, nearly pulling her towards the quarters where they could stay.

Annaisha had never shared her body with a man before, but something about Zhanshi made her want to learn new things.

"Zip," Zhanshi told to the bot who followed them, "we need you to go to the library and gather all of the known routes to the planetoid."

"Right away."

Annaisha knew that Zhanshi had asked Zip to do it so that they could get a little privacy. He was obviously much better at all of this than she was. Zhanshi used one of the passes that Meizhen had given them to open the door.

"This is one of the deluxe

quarters. It has a holo-deck just like the one in the spaceship."

Annaisha walked with him into the holo-deck room. The goggles were a lot bigger there, and Annaisha put her set over her head. Zhanshi, still holding Annaisha, turned on the system so that they were back on Zhongguo. Holo-decks were expensive to run, and Annaisha didn't get the opportunity to use them that often.

"Where are we going?"

"To a place that I've never shown anyone else."

Annaisha waited for the system to boot up and take them to their destination.

Suddenly, she was underwater.

"Where is this?"

"Under the waves, Annaisha. This is my most private place. It's where I go to think."

She moved to him and tilted her head so that she could kiss him with their goggles on. Despite twisting, she hit his VR goggles with her own.

"Sorry!" Annaisha felt incredibly embarrassed for trying to kiss him while they both had goggles on.

Annaisha felt Zhanshi pull the goggles off of her face before putting his big hands on her waist and drawing her close to him, as close as they'd been on the dance floor. He leaned her head back with a hand in her hair and kissed her tenderly.

"I think that we're done with the holo-deck."

Zhanshi picked Annaisha up in his arms before he brought her back to the bedroom. She loved the look in his eyes, as if a fire were burning him inside.

"I want to see your body," Zhanshi said. "Show me."

Annaisha knew that she didn't have a perfect body. She was too curvy. Her insecurity made her not want to get undressed in front of him.

"Come here," he commanded softly. Annaisha got closer to him. His hands went inside of her clothes and tugged them off quickly, until Annaisha was standing in front him totally naked.

His head bent to take one of her nipples into his mouth, then his hand went to the other breast while his second hand went to the small of her back, as if she might run away.

Streaks of lightning filled her body while he sucked on her breasts. As he was rolling the nipple of the other breast, she was getting wet. Very wet.

The whole world tilted just as it had when she was on the spaceship while it was going through the asteroid belt, but this time she landed on her back on the bed. Zhanshi was pushing her thighs apart and settling his head between them.

She could feel herself getting tense. She was in a completely vulnerable position, and she didn't know if she liked it.

But with the first touch of his tongue to her lower lips, she felt as if she were on fire, as if his tongue was a paintbrush that was spreading pure fire.

"Oh," she moaned, arching her back. "Ah."

Zhanshi didn't have any response besides flicking his tongue a little faster. She panted hard when she thrashed her head around, barely able to stand the intensity of the feeling of Zhanshi's tongue between her thighs.

"Take me," she begged. "Please."

Zhanshi pushed himself into a different position, throwing her legs over his shoulders.

"What do you want?"

"You," she whispered.

He touched the tip of his cock

to her entrance.

"Like this?"

"Inside."

He pushed in just a

centimeter.

"That's what you want, isn't

it?"

"More," she growled. She might

be somewhat physically powerless

while her legs were over his

shoulders, but she wasn't going to

stand being teased for much longer. She bucked her hips and captured just a little more of his hard rod.

Then he sank all the way into her. There was a flash of burning sensation, where she felt like she was being stretched larger than anyone or anything had ever stretched her before. She was helpless beneath him as he drove inside of her body over and over again, her legs providing support as he pounded inside of her.

Then she watched his face tighten as his orgasm approached.

"Ugh," he said, as warmth filled and spread throughout her insides.

Then he pulled out and held her in his arms.

"Thank you," she whispered. "That was wonderful."

He kissed her cheek before kissing her mouth.

"Anytime."

News

Annaisha

The next morning, Zip was back in their room. If he thought anything about Zhanshi and Annaisha sleeping in the same bed, he wasn't saying anything. Then again, bots weren't as judgmental as normal society. Ribenren kept their intimate moments extremely private, so

Annaisha felt very shy about Zip being with them, but he was almost an extension of herself.

"I have some news, Annaisha."

She yawned. She was totally naked, but AI didn't care about nudity, or so she hoped.

"Go ahead."

"Meizhen asked me to contact that AI on Xenkaku. Every time I tried, all I got were rejected access codes."

The panic surging in

Annaisha's veins woke her up more effectively than ice water could.

"Let's try the back door. Zip, listen carefully to the numbers of the back door."

Zip listened to her and sent over the access code.

"We're in."

"Welcome, KSM agent," the speakers on Zip said, "You are granted limited access for your mission. We are happy to comply with Intergalactic Federation protocols. Thank you for coming."

"We're in. Tell Meizhen to meet us so that I can take her out for a good dinner."

"Yes, Your Highness." Zip sent a comm mail to Meizhen.

Meizhen might not be an actual space marine, but she could do a lot with the clearance of one against whatever strange codes the foul king had programmed into Annaisha's system.

The prince was happy with the

way that things had progressed. Somehow, he looked at each obstacle as an opportunity. He acted as if it had been a foregone conclusion that Meizhen could fix things while their normal resources couldn't.

A comm mail dinged. Zip pulled it up on his main screen.

Annaisha read the gist out loud: "We're going to eat with Meizhen and her friend Huizhong."

"Sounds good to me."

"Let's go, then. Are you feeling hungover?"

"No. I don't really drink."

"Great. We're supposed to be there in ten minutes."

Meal

Zhanshi

Zhanshi brought Annaisha into a small room off of one of the dining facilities. Meizhen already had a presentation set up and Huizhong had a small portable computer out in front of her.

"I'm so glad that you're here. Let's go over the plan."

Without anything else, Meizhen

began to outline the steps of her plan, showing them each part. Zhanshi listened to all of it with one arm around Annaisha's shoulders. She put her head on his shoulder. Her smell was intoxicating and very distracting.

"I'm sure that I can at least stop the progress of the virus, but developing a cure could take an incredible amount of time. Annaisha's bot makes it clear that the virus is low-grade but powerful and very obviously implanted."

"I agree," Huizhong told her. "But I know that we can find a solution."

"Please try." Annaisha yawned.

"Go get some rest," Meizhen told her kindly.

Annaisha and Zhanshi got to their feet.

"Thank you for your work," they told her. "We really appreciate it."

"Forget about it," Meizhen said.

"Just pay it forward at some point."

Annaisha, Zip, and Zhanshi walked back to their rooms. This time, before Zhanshi could, Zip suggested the very thing that Zhanshi had the night before.

"I'll go to the library for a few hours."

Annaisha and Zhanshi held hands while they walked the rest of the way back. Annaisha liked sharing a bed with Zhanshi, but she also enjoyed sleep.

Today, sleep was going to win.

"Zhanshi, I'm exhausted."

"I've worn you out, is that it?"

"Pretty much."

"I'll just hold you tonight. I promise." He leaned in to kiss her temple. Her arms came around him. She kissed deeply but way too briefly.

He put his hand on her cheek, feeling the velvet-soft skin. He knew that his father would always be his father, but he'd chose

Annaisha any day.

Tactics

Annaisha

The following day, they were making their way to the space docks to meet with Meizhen.

A man with black professor's robes stepped forward.

"Excuse me…what are your kind doing here? I'll need to see your student pass."

They handed him their passes.

He scrutinized them carefully.

"I'll have to call it in."

Zhanshi and Annaisha began to run. The guards stood still for a moment before going to chase them.

"Anti-surveillance tactics!" Zhanshi said while they ran. They went in and around business buildings. Annaisha worried that Meizhen would think that they had abandoned her.

But then she saw Meizhen's

face on the inside of a spacecraft.

"Zhanshi, I think that she's over there."

"You're right. Let's go." They weren't able to sprint anymore, so they jogged slowly towards the spacecraft. Ramps came shooting out, and Annaisha and Zhanshi ran into the spaceship before the guards could get them.

Then the ramp was retracting and the spaceship was moving smoothly through the air. They were safe now.

"Let's follow the most direct route to Xenkaku," Zhanshi told Meizhen. "We have to get there as quickly as we can."

"But the most direct route goes near disputed territory. There's a war going on over there."

"Are you sure that there isn't another path?"

"No. We need to arrive as soon as possible to save your planetoid from the damage that the virus has already caused. You think that it's limited to some of your bots, but it will soon take over all of them. It was planted by Sangui in order to shut your entire park down."

Annaisha felt tears threaten, but she held them back. "I understand."

"Strap in," Zhanshi ordered. "We're going on a wild ride."

Annaisha strapped herself in and saw that Zip was attaching himself to the wall like he had before. He had a keen sense of self-preservation, which was good considering just how much he had cost. While she was strapped down, she fell asleep.

* * *

An alarm chimed.

"What was that?"

"We just passed a cloaked ship." Zhanshi touched some things on the control panel which made an image appear on the screen. It was just a blob, but it was enough to make him flick some other switches.

"We're going into hyperdrive."

"Isn't hyperdrive incredibly dangerous because you can crash into space debris at a higher velocity?"

"Yes."

With that, Annaisha was pushed back into her chair by the g-force of the spaceship. She knew that he was a good pilot, but she didn't know if he was good enough to keep them alive. Running into space debris at a high velocity could irreparably damage their ship and doom them to death in the vacuum of space.

But he quickly darted around every obstacle, shaking the other ship. They couldn't see the blob anymore. They probably weren't completely gone, just left behind in their space dust.

Meizhen's ship might have seemed like easy prey for a space

pirate, but they weren't meek little bunnies just waiting to be eaten. With Zhanshi by her side, she knew that she'd be on the side of the angels.

Her heart was still thumping a little faster than usual when Annaisha saw Meizhen and Zhanshi exchange a high-five.

Annaisha was sure that Zhanshi would've spilled a lot of blood to get them free, but he didn't have to. He truly was a champion, though.

Arrival on Xenkaku

Zhanshi

Zhanshi sighed when they got within a closer range of Xenkaku. He could see the brilliant red of his father's flagship from this distance.

"What's wrong?"

"My father is definitely here." Zhanshi hated to admit that there was the tiniest part of him which hoped that his father was more honorable than he really was. "And he brought friends."

On the screen of the spaceship, Zhanshi zoomed in on Xenkaku's space dock. There were smaller spaceships around the king's own. Zhanshi's blood burned to see them docked on Annaisha's home.

Meizhen brought an image of the planetoid up on her screen.

"What are you looking at?"

"I'm doing a search through all the code in your mainframes."

"But that would take forever...it takes an enormous amount of processing capacity."

Meizhen patted her control panel. "What do you think my ship can do? Just fly?"

Annaisha blinked for a few seconds, then Meizhen said. "Look at the red parts."

Zhanshi looked at the map of Xenkaku that Meizhen had pulled up. "What are the red parts?"

"Places where the mal-code has

infected Xenkaku's computers, including the ones in the robots."

"Can we fix it remotely?"

"We can try."

"Just use the back door that I programmed for KSM."

Annaisha typed in the code.

ACCESS DENIED.

"Why isn't it working? Did I press the wrong button?" Annaisha typed in the back door access code a second time.

ACCESS DENIED.

"Let me try something."

Meizhen typed and typed into the control panel, trying to get in.

"What kind of coder could shut down a KSM code?" Annaisha paced around the room, muttering curses about Zhanshi's father the whole time.

Zhanshi didn't mind. His father deserved everything that she was saying and more. He was much more worried about Annaisha.

"I can't get in," Meizhen sighed. "Not the fast way."

"Hold on." Zhanshi turned back to the computer. "If this doesn't do it, I don't know what will."

Zhanshi knew his father. He had incredible difficulty remembering pass codes, so he used the same one for everything, the same one he'd seen him enter so many times. If Zhanshi was an obedient heir, he would stop there.

But he might as well use the pass codes now. Nobody knew that he had them, but the royal operating system that his father installed on Xenkaku's system should respond to them.

His fingers moved so fast that they blurred.

ACCESS GRANTED.

He had gained access to Annaisha's dock entrance.

Exiting the Spaceship

Annaisha

Arriving on the dock, the five of them exited the spaceship carefully. Zhanshi, Huizhong, and Meizhen were armed and ready for trouble. Everyone was wearing a shield suit, including Zip, but Annaisha was far from scared. A wave of cold fury had taken over her body since she'd been locked out of her own planetoid system, and it wasn't responding to her telepathic nudges. She wasn't a very strong telepath, true, but she'd always been able to hear the AI in her head if she thought hard enough. Now she couldn't.

She gritted her teeth. The king was going to pay.

The three armed members of the party created a formation around Annaisha and Zip. The heroes were quiet as they made

their way to the heart of
Annaisha's planetoid, listening for
any sound at all, with fingers on
the triggers of their laser guns.

They got to a door which
Zhanshi opened with his father's
code.

Meizhen brought out a small
tablet and connected it to
Xenkaku's mainframe, her fingers
flitting furiously as she hacked the
system. A minute later, she gave
them a thumbs up.

Zhanshi reached to open the door leading into the control room of the space dock, but it was locked. Meizhen ran over, her tablet gripped in her hand.

"I can't make it open."

The Zhongguoren had noticed that they had arrived. They had their own hacker fighting back.

"I'm sorry, Annaisha, but I would need more time to force my way in. We're locked out."

Tears pricking her eyes,

Annaisha began to call in her head to her sick droids, her will creating power as she felt traces of their energy. Her telepathy wasn't all that reliable. Tears flowed down her cheeks and to her chin as she encouraged them to find the strength to rise up and block all but the main entrance and exit.

This time, unlike the last, she could feel them moving from her telepathic connection.

Be ready, she told them.

Flicker

Annaisha

Annaisha stared as the lights flickered around her, her energy field short circuiting.

"Wow. Pretty cool."

Then a door clicked open. Meizhen gave another thumbs up. Zhanshi took Annaisha's hand, leading her in as she slipped out of her trance.

The king was just inside of the door.

Annaisha lunged forward and began to shout.

"You are trespassing on my queendom!" It was just a planetoid, it was true, but she was the queen of her family's territory. They were a very small part of Riben, but they had autonomy. She didn't exercise her right to rule, but she was outraged that Zhanshi's father, the king, would try to infringe upon her rightful place.

Zhanshi just watched, knowing that his father had no pride to protect. He had been a space pirate in his younger days, and everyone knew it. Zhanshi eyed the door leading into the main entryway.

When Annaisha paused for breath — still needing a lot of fuel to keep yelling at his father — he asked, "Is that door made of Ptunian metal?"

Zhanshi grinned from his idea.

He leaned in to whisper in her ear, "Speak to it. We could use it as a prison for my father when we're done."

He watched as fire blazed in Annaisha's eyes, and she set her scorching gaze on the king.

Strips of metal peeled off and positioned around the king. He shouted, "To me! Apprehend the intruders."

But Zhanshi wasn't a galactic champion for nothing. The three people in the squad used their weapons to immediately subdue the king's guard. They were no match for a champion.

"Thank you," Annaisha said, throwing herself into Zhanshi's arms despite the blood on his uniform. She tilted her face up for his kiss, and he bent down and kissed her hard.

"Secure my father."

Annaisha turned and stared at the strips of Ptunian metal around the king.

"Tighten up," she told them.

It imprisoned the king in a small jail cell, but he began to laugh uncontrollably despite his confinement.

"What's so funny, Father?" Zhanshi thought that his father would be furious to be captured like this.

"I can see the blue in the strips. The planetoid is losing power."

Zhanshi saw Annaisha's eyes widen with horror.

"They're shutting down my planetoid!" she shouted. "We need to fix it right away."

"Tell the metal to open a door to the core of the planetoid. I can run fast enough to get there in time."

Annaisha was crying now, but she closed her eyes and asked for the Ptunian metal's help.

The metal peeled back,

creating an opening only just a little too narrow for Zhanshi to push himself through. He pulled at it, helping it tear faster. He finally got through and ran for the core.

Gleam

Annaisha

With some of the metal helping Zhanshi, Annaisha could see the king more clearly. She noticed a glow in the pocket of his cloak.

"Stars above," she whispered as she hurried over and reached into the small cage to snatch it out. She ran after Zhanshi, shouting to him when she realized that she wouldn't be able to run fast enough to catch him.

"I have the power core," she bellowed. "Turn back!"

Zhanshi made a gesture for her to throw it to him. She stopped in her tracks. Throwing the core was a tremendous risk. People died that way; her entire planetoid would die if the core was dropped and the nuclear energy from it spread everywhere. She would lose everything if she even survived.

"What if you drop it?"

"I'm a galactic champion," Zhanshi told her, his dimples deepening.

Annaisha hurled the power core at him with as much precision as she could muster. She stopped breathing until she saw it in his hand. Then he was running forward as fast as he could go.

Annaisha's heart thumped hard after a series of horrifying creaks and crashes began to shake the planetoid around her. She didn't know if Zhanshi would be able to make it in time. She clenched her fists and prayed to the stars above that Zhanshi would be able to make it.

But no sooner had she closed her eyes than the funny noises stopped. Annaisha could see Zhanshi going back on the stairs, giving Annaisha a smoldering grin. He climbed back up to her and brought her back to Meizhen and

Huizhong.

Meizhen said, "I'm glad that you're back. Let's go check on your droids."

Epilogue

Zhanshi

Zhanshi sat on the throne and surveyed his kingdom. After his father's arrest, he'd been able to ascend to the throne and take his father's crown. A tape of the battle had been linked on the Net and all of the records that Zhanshi had been able to download had brought his father under the scrutiny of the

Galactic courts. Because his father had attempted to prevent his son from ever gaining a foothold in the kingdom's power, he'd accidentally handed him the whole kingdom.

Queen Annaisha was preparing her planetoid for a move to a new star system when an expansion was planned. They'd already started marketing it in the quadrant. For some reason, Zhanshi and Annaisha were inexplicably popular. Everyone was waiting for the baby who was growing inside of Annaisha. She complained about being kicked in the ribs, but Zhanshi knew that she loved their baby to bits.

She was overdue by two weeks. The baby's mixed Zhongguoren and Ribenren heritage made the healers uncertain when the baby would come, but the baby's gestation period was two weeks beyond the longer Ribenren period.

Zip came up to Zhanshi.

"What is it, Zip?"

"Annaisha is giving birth."

Zhanshi got to his feet. "Take me to her."

He followed Annaisha's beloved bot into the infirmary. Annaisha had insisted on received just the same care as any of their subjects, so she was in a bed beside all the other pregnant ladies.

"How are you doing, love?"

Her hand was on her stomach. There was sweat all over her

forehead. Her hair was sticking to it.

"Ouch," she moaned. Zhanshi guessed that her answer was the best one that she could give.

"I'm right here, Annaisha." She squeezed his hand so hard that she might have cracked a bone. He tried not to wince.

He could see the spikes of her contractions. She writhed uncomfortably on the bed, her face going red.

"I can see the baby's head," the midwife announced. While Annaisha's lower parts were some of Zhanshi's favorite body parts, he didn't look. There were things going on down there that he never wanted to see, as much as he loved his wife and their child.

"Ah!" his wife screamed. Zhanshi felt her hand clench painfully hard around his own.

"You've done it," the midwife praised. She pulled the baby into her arms and bustled away to the medi-couch, so that it could clean up the baby.

"You did it," Zhanshi said to Annaisha. "How are you?"

"Exhausted. But it was worth it." Both of them didn't look at the mess on the bedsheets. "Thank you for rushing to my side. Everything happened so fast. I didn't even think that my stomach cramps were contractions until Zip nudged me towards going to the infirmary."

He leaned in to kiss her mouth.

"Do you want to hold your baby?" The midwife was beside them with a clean baby in her arms. She was apparently used to married couples kissing in the labor and delivery section of the infirmary.

Zhanshi accepted the baby in his arms.

"So beautiful." He looked at his

baby's sweet little mouth. The baby was sleeping the pure sleep of the innocent.

"I'll protect you forever," he promised his child, whose soft weight in his arms meant everything.

"I love you," Annaisha said softly.

"I love you, too."

THE END

Notes

Teppanyaki - a Riben grill that is used for fast and easy cooking

Okonomiyaki - a flat pancake-like food, sort of like an omelette

Takoyaki - fried balls partly made with octopus (one of my favorite foods ever)

Galixia - a large planetoid that has switched into the hands of Silexa, one of the members of the Intergalactic Federation

Zhongguo - a large planet with many men who have dark hair and sometimes glowing golden skin

Zhongguoren - the race that lives on Zhongguo

Zhongwen - the native language of Zhongguo, though nearly everyone speaks and reads Standard

Riben - a smaller member of the Intergalactic Federation, known for its cutting-edge technology, especially when it comes to robots. It's a wealthy planet, though not very big.

Meizhen - a hacker. Her name means beautiful pearl.

Xenkaku - the disputed planetoid which Annaisha owns and runs.

Cover designs and developmental editing by Lux Development

Final editing provided by Heatwave Books

www.ingramcontent.com/pod-product-compliance
Lightning Source LLC
Chambersburg PA
CBHW060940030726
47503CB00003B/668